TIME HUNTERS

OUTBACK OUTLAW

First published in Great Britain by HarperCollins *Children's Books* in 2014
HarperCollins *Children's Books* is a division of HarperCollins*Publishers* Ltd,
77–85 Fulham Palace Road, Hammersmith, London, W6 8JB.

The HarperCollins website address is: www.harpercollins.co.uk

1
Text © Hothouse Fiction Limited 2014
Illustrations © HarperCollins *Children's Books*, 2014
Illustrations by Dynamo

ISBN 978-0-00-754998-6

Printed and bound in England by Clays Ltd, St Ives plc

MIX
Paper from
responsible sources
FSC™ C007454

FSC™ is a non-profit international organisation established to promote
the responsible management of the world's forests. Products carrying the
FSC label are independently certified to assure consumers that they come
from forests that are managed to meet the social, economic and
ecological needs of present and future generations,
and other controlled sources.

Find out more about HarperCollins and the environment at
www.harpercollins.co.uk/green

CHRIS BLAKE

TiME HUNTERS

OUTBACK OUTLAW

HarperCollins *Children's Books*

Travel through time with Tom
on more

adventures!

Gladiator Clash

Knight Quest

Viking Raiders

Greek Warriors

Pirate Mutiny

Egyptian Curse

Cowboy Showdown

Samurai Assassin

Outback Outlaw

Stone Age Rampage

Mohican Brave

Aztec Attack

For games, competitions and more visit:

www.time-hunters.com

CONTENTS

With special thanks to Martin Howard

PROLOGUE

1500 AD, Mexico

As far as Zuma was concerned, there were only two good things about being a human sacrifice. One was the lovely black pendant the tribal elders had given her to wear. The other was the little Chihuahua dog the high priest had just placed next to her.

I've always wanted a pet, thought Zuma, as the trembling pup snuggled up close. *Though this does seem like an extreme way to get one.*

Zuma lay on an altar at the top of the Great Pyramid. In honour of the mighty Aztec rain god, Tlaloc, she'd been painted bright blue and wore a feathered headdress.

The entire village had turned out to watch the slave girl being sacrificed in exchange for plentiful rainfall and a good harvest. She could see her master strutting in the crowd below, proud to have supplied the slave for today's sacrifice. He looked a little relieved too. And Zuma couldn't blame him. As slaves went, she was a troublesome one, always trying to run away. But she couldn't help it – her greatest dream was to be free!

Zuma had spent the entire ten years of her life in slavery, and she was sick of it. She knew she should be honoured to be a sacrifice, but she had a much better plan – to escape!

"Besides," she said, frowning at her painted skin, "blue is not my colour!"

"Hush, slave!" said the high priest, Acalan, his face hidden by a jade mask. "The ceremony is about to begin." He raised his knife in the air.

"Shame I'll be missing it," said Zuma. "Tell Tlaloc I'd like to take a *rain* check." As the priest lowered the knife, she pulled up her knees and kicked him hard in the stomach with both feet.

"*Oof!*" The priest doubled over, clutching his belly. The blade clattered to the floor.

Zuma rolled off the altar, dodging the other priests, who fell over each other in their attempts to catch her. One priest jumped into her path, but the little Chihuahua dog sank his teeth into the man's ankle. As the priest howled in pain, Zuma whistled to the dog.

"Nice work, doggie!" she said. "I'm getting

out of here and you're coming with me!" She scooped him up and dashed down the steps of the pyramid.

"Grab her!" groaned the high priest from above.

Many hands reached out to catch the slave girl, but Zuma was fast and determined. She bolted towards the jungle bordering the pyramid. Charging into the cool green leaves, she ran until she could no longer hear the shouts of the crowd.

"We did it," she said to the dog. "We're free!"

As she spoke, the sky erupted in a loud rumble of thunder, making the dog yelp. "Thunder's nothing to be scared of," said Zuma.

"Don't be so sure about that!" came a deep voice above her.

Zuma looked up to see a creature with blue skin and long, sharp fangs, like a jaguar. He carried a wooden drum and wore a feathered headdress, just like Zuma's.

She knew at once who it was. "Tlaloc!" she gasped.

The rain god's bulging eyes glared down at her. "You have dishonoured me!" he bellowed. "No sacrifice has ever escaped before!"

"Really? I'm the first?" Zuma beamed

with pride, but the feeling didn't last long. Tlaloc's scowl was too scary. "I'm sorry!" she said quietly. "I just wanted to be free."

"You will *never* be free!" Tlaloc hissed. "Unless you can escape again…"

Tlaloc banged his drum, and thunder rolled through the jungle.

He pounded the drum a second time, and thick black clouds gathered high above the treetops.

"This isn't looking good," Zuma whispered. Holding the dog tightly, she closed her eyes.

On the third deafening drum roll, the jungle floor began to shake and a powerful force tugged at Zuma. She felt her whole body being swallowed up inside… the drum!

CHAPTER 1

SHOWSTOPPER

Tom Sullivan peeked round the curtain at the side of the stage. His school talent show had just started and he was helping out behind the scenes. On stage a girl from Tom's class was singing a pop song – badly. Beside Tom, Zuma put her hands over her ears.

"Ouch!" the Aztec slave girl complained. "She sounds like a howler monkey with a sore tooth!"

Tom grinned. In her feathered headdress and blue skin paint, Zuma looked ready to take to the stage herself. Chilli, the tiny Chihuahua dog in Zuma's arms, yapped in agreement. Tom had to be careful not to say anything in reply. The backstage area was crammed with performers getting ready for their turn in the spotlight, but Tom was the only person who could see Zuma and Chilli.

"Watch out!" Tom told a group of dancers called Break Quake. "Someone spilled a drink on the floor. It's slippery." He pointed to a small puddle on the floor and pushed back the stage scenery, giving Break Quake some space.

Zuma watched the dancers warm up. Only a week had passed since Tom had beaten an Aztec drum in his dad's museum, accidentally freeing Zuma and Chilli from it. Since then, the three of them had travelled through time looking for six golden coins hidden by the fearsome rain god, Tlaloc. So far, they had visited the Wild West and Medieval Japan, and found two of the coins. If they recovered all six, Zuma would win back her freedom.

On stage, the singer took a bow and the audience clapped. Tom pulled a rope and the curtain came down. "OK. You're next," he told Break Quake. "Take your places. Ten seconds."

The dancers rushed past, jostling Mr Jenkins the caretaker, who had arrived with a mop and bucket to clean up the puddle.

Mr Braintree the drama teacher, walked out in front of the curtain. "Next, we have the *amazing* Break Quake dance group. Let's give them a very warm welcome…"

The clapping grew louder. Some of the audience began whistling and stamping their feet. Backstage, Tom switched on the music and tugged the rope to lift the curtain. The dancers ran on stage and started their routine.

"I wish people could see me," Zuma said, tickling Chilli's ears. "I've got heaps of talent. I could have won this competition standing on my head."

"Oh yeah?" whispered Tom, out of the side of his mouth. "How?" Zuma had been brave and clever during their adventures, but she hadn't shown Tom a special talent.

"For your information, I'm a fantastic gymnast," said Zuma "Watch this!" She put Chilli on the floor, took a step forward and launched herself into a handstand.

Right where the caretaker had just
mopped the floor.

Zuma squealed as her hand slipped on
the wet surface. She toppled into Tom,
who stepped back into Mr Jenkins's bucket,
knocking it over and sending soapy water
flooding out across the stage. Immediately,

one of Break Quake skidded and crashed
into another dancer. Both of them landed on
top of a girl, who was spinning on her back
at the front of the stage. As the dancers slid
about, Mr Braintree rushed on stage to help,
only to lose his footing and go tumbling to
the floor. The performance was ruined.

"Oh noooo!" Tom moaned. As Mr Braintree looked over towards him, the teacher saw the overturned bucket at Tom's feet. His eyes narrowed.

Behind Tom, Zuma had picked herself up, a guilty expression on her face. She grabbed a rope and pulled on it. Everyone was staring at Tom in stunned silence, so no one noticed when the curtain seemed to come down on its own.

Mr Braintree stood up and wiped bubbles from his eyes. Break Quake were slowly getting back to their feet. All of them were glaring at Tom. They walked offstage without a word.

"We'll talk about this later," Mr Braintree growled at Tom. "Right now, we've got a show to save." He disappeared in the same direction as the dancers.

Zuma looked at Tom and smiled
nervously. "I'm… er… I'm sorry," she said.

Tom picked up the bucket. "So, you're a
brilliant gymnast, are you?" he said glumly.

"I forgot about the wet floor," Zuma
mumbled. "I'm really sorry."

Tom sighed. "At least things can't get any
worse," he said.

At that moment, thunder rumbled across
the stage. A cloud appeared over Tom's

head. A narrow rainstorm began to fall on him like a spotlight. He groaned.

"I think you spoke too soon," said Zuma.

Together, they looked up. Rolling clouds had blotted out the stage lights. Tlaloc's face appeared in the clouds, his eyes bulging angrily.

The rain god opened his mouth to speak, revealing a line of sharp fangs. "I see you are shaking with fear, mortal," he bellowed.

Trying not to show his fear, Tom stood up straight. "Actually, I'm laughing at how silly you look," he replied.

Tlaloc snarled. "Soon you *will* be quivering with terror," he hissed between clenched fangs. "You have been lucky so far, but luck cannot last forever. You will never find the next gold coin. Zuma is doomed!"

A sparkling mist rose up and a swirling

wind blew across the stage. Glancing at Zuma, Tom saw she was holding Chilli tightly. Tlaloc's strange mist swirled round him, and then the stage began to disappear as they travelled through the tunnels of time.

CHAPTER 2

DANGER DOWN UNDER

Suddenly, the mist vanished. Tom blinked.
Shading his eyes from the fierce sun, he
saw he was standing in a field of dry-
looking grass with a few trees dotted
about. Low, craggy hills stretched into the
distance. The ground was red and dusty
beneath his feet. Everywhere Tom looked
there were sheep – hundreds and hundreds
of sheep. He had never seen so many sheep
in his life.

"Phew, it's hot!" said Zuma. "Where are we?"

Tom turned round. The Aztec girl was still holding on to Chilli, but the blue paint was gone. She was wearing cord trousers, dusty boots and a long-sleeved shirt with a waistcoat over the top. Her feathered headdress had also vanished. In its place was a large straw hat. Zuma's long black hair was pulled back into a ponytail. The only thing that hadn't changed was the black pendant that hung round her neck.

Looking down, Tom saw he was wearing a similar outfit. He thought hard. History was his favourite subject, but their clothes didn't tell him much about where Tlaloc had sent them this time. "I'm not sure," he said. "Or when. People have been wearing trousers, shirts and waistcoats for hundreds of years."

"So much for your amazing brain power. Maybe we could—" Zuma stopped talking and squealed. "Hey, what's *that* thing?"

Tom spun round. A grin spread across his face as he saw an animal bouncing across the field. "*That*," he laughed, "is a kangaroo. Which means we're in Australia, and explains why it's so hot."

"Aus-where?" Zuma looked puzzled.

"Australia. It's a big continent on the other side of the world from Mexico," said Tom. His face lit up with excitement. "I've always wanted to go there. Everyone says it's amazing. It's got loads of plants and animals you can't find anywhere else in the world and—"

Zuma held up a hand to stop him. "Don't get carried away, Brains," she said. "We're here to find my coin, not for a holiday."

"OK, OK," said Tom. "Shall we start by asking your necklace for help?"

Zuma nodded. The black pendant round her neck was magical. The stone gave them clues about where to find Tlaloc's golden coins. She held up the pendant and said the rhyme that made the stone work:

"Mirror, mirror, on a chain,
Can you help us? Please explain!
We are lost and must be told
How to find the coins of gold."

Tom and Zuma huddled over the necklace, waiting for a reply. Sure enough, spidery silver writing began to appear on the surface of the black disc:

In a time when outlaws raised a cheer,
Look for the man who knows no fear.
Listen out for a merry song
Follow the trail to the billabong.
Now that you are getting warm,
Seek out the loud bang in a storm.
Four more coins and then you're free
The swag's beneath a cabbage tree.

Zuma groaned. "Just once it'd be nice if it told us *where* to find the coin, rather than talking in riddles."

Tom grinned. "That would be too simple," he said. "Plus it's fun trying to work out what they mean. Who do you think 'the man who knows no fear' is?"

"Maybe it's him," Zuma replied. She pointed to a man in the next field.

"I'm sure Tlaloc won't have made it that

easy," said Tom.

"It's worth a try," Zuma told him. "Even horrible angry rain gods like Tlaloc make mistakes sometimes."

Tom and Zuma walked across the stubbly field towards the man Zuma had spotted. Chilli ran at a sheep, barking. Then he quickly jumped into Zuma's arms when it charged.

"Don't worry, Chilli," Tom laughed. "That sheep's never seen a Chihuahua before – he doesn't know how tough and brave you can be."

The sun beat down and Tom was glad of the straw hat shading his face. As they got closer to the man, Tom saw he was holding a sheep between his legs. With expert hands he was snipping off the animal's wool with large, odd-looking scissors. Next to him was a pile of fleeces.

"Hey there!" Zuma called, as they got closer. "We're looking for the man who knows no fear."

The sheep shearer looked confused. "You what?"

"The man who—" Zuma began.

"Maybe you could just point us in the direction of the nearest town," Tom interrupted.

"It's that way," said the man. He scratched his chin and pointed. "You can't miss it – it's the only place for miles with more than two buildings."

The walk took almost an hour under the hot Australian sun. Tom and Zuma often had to push through flocks of sheep that refused to move out of their way. By the time they arrived at the town they were thirsty and tired.

"I hope they have somewhere to cool off," said Zuma, as they walked down the street.

"I'd love a glass of cold water," said Tom.

"Forget a glass of cold water," muttered Zuma. "I want to stand under a great big waterfall."

Tom looked round, scratching his head. The Australian town was small and looked a lot like the places he and Zuma had seen in the Wild West. The shops and buildings were made of wood, and all had covered walkways in front to shade the townsfolk from the sun. The street was nothing but dusty, baked earth. It was completely empty.

"Where is everyone?" Tom asked.

Zuma shrugged. "Maybe there's a waterfall round here after all."

It wasn't long before Tom's question was answered. At the other end of the street a group of people appeared. They were walking slowly with their hands in the air. Behind them were three men wearing shabby, dirty clothes. All three looked like they needed a shave. And each was holding a gun.

"Listen up!" one shouted. "Do what you're told and no one gets hurt."

Before they could be spotted, Zuma grabbed Tom's sleeve and pulled him into a grocery store.

"I think it's a hold-up," Tom whispered. "Those men look like they're taking the whole town hostage! They must be outlaws. Let's get out of here before they find us too."

"But what about my coin?" Zuma hissed back.

"We'll worry about the coin later," said Tom.

Zuma nodded. With Chilli at their heels, they began to creep away. "Follow me," said Tom, leading Zuma into a narrow alley. "We can hide here."

"Sorry, mate. I don't think you can," said a gruff voice.

Tom gulped as a sandy-haired man with grizzly stubble stepped out in front of them. In the man's hands was a pistol. It was pointing straight at them.

Tom and Zuma walked backwards out of the alley, raising their hands. "Don't shoot, we're just travellers," said Tom quickly.

"You picked the wrong day to visit this town, traveller," said the man, with a sneer.

"What's going on?" asked Zuma. "Who are you?"

The outlaw spat on the ground. Turning his gun on Zuma he said, "Well, missy, I'm Dusty Moore. I belong to Brave Ben Hall's outback gang. You and your friend here are my hostages. Now move it!"

CHAPTER 3

PARTY TIME

Tom and Zuma marched down the main
street with their hands in the air. Dusty
Moore followed closely behind, keeping his
gun trained on them. Halfway down the
road was a large building. Painted on the
wooden front was the word 'Hotel'. A crowd
of townsfolk stood outside, surrounded by the
outlaw gang. On the steps of the hotel, Tom
saw a tall man with a bristling black beard.
He had a sack slung over his shoulder, and a

knife with a gleaming silver blade tucked into his belt.

The man raised his hat. "Ladies and gentlemen," he shouted, "my name is Ben Hall. Some call me 'Brave' Ben Hall. You may have heard of me."

"We've heard of you, all right," yelled a man in the crowd. "You're a thief and an outlaw. You're under arrest. Come quietly and there won't be any trouble."

Ben Hall chuckled. "Is that a policeman?" he said. "I don't much like policemen. Too busy hassling ordinary folk. Bill, Jimmy, take that man down the station and lock him up in his own cells. Make sure you throw away the key."

Whooping and laughing, two of the outlaws pulled the policeman out of the crowd and pushed him roughly down the street. Tom glanced nervously at Zuma. With the town's policeman behind bars, there was no one to help them now. He was surprised to see the Aztec girl smiling.

"*Brave* Ben Hall," she whispered. "Maybe he's the man who knows no fear."

Tom's eyes widened. Zuma could be right. Before he could reply, Ben Hall jerked his thumb towards the main door of the hotel. "Now we've got rid of the lawman, I'd like to invite you all inside," he said.

The crowd of people had no choice. They filed into the hotel at gunpoint. Tom and Zuma followed everyone else. They found themselves in a large plain room with a long wooden bar. Ben Hall jumped on top of it and nodded to an old woman at a piano in the corner. Immediately, she began playing a jaunty tune.

"You can put away those guns now, boys," Ben Hall called out to his men.

The outlaw gang grinned and stuck their guns in their belts. Tom frowned. What kind of robbery was this?

Pushing his hat back on his head, Ben Hall reached into his sack and pulled out a fistful of money and gold and glittering jewellery. The crowd gasped in astonishment. Zuma's eyes lit up at the sight of the sparkling gems.

"Good people," yelled Ben Hall with a grin, "me and my lads just robbed a rich, greedy landowner. This wealth belongs to the entire town. To celebrate, I'm throwing a party!"

Dropping the money and jewels back into the sack, he tossed it across the room. Behind Tom and Zuma, Dusty Moore caught it.

"Put that somewhere safe, Dusty," Ben told him. "We'll share it out later."

The hotel shook with loud cheers and stamping feet. The old woman at the piano thumped the keys, filling the room with loud music. A fiddler joined in. Arm in arm, couples began dancing. Singing along to the music, Ben Hall jumped behind the bar and used his knife to open bottles, before handing out drinks to everyone. The kitchen door flew open and trays heaped with food were bought out for the partygoers.

Within minutes, the party was in full swing. Zuma, unable to resist, did a somersault and backflipped her way across the room. Tom stared at her. The Aztec girl really *was* a fantastic gymnast! Darting through the crowd, Chilli jumped up at the laughing townsfolk, wagging his tail until they

rewarded him with chunks of roasted meat.

Only one person wasn't smiling. Dusty
Moore pushed his way through the crowd
with a scowl on his face. In his hand was the

precious bag of loot. Spotting a new friend,
Chilli ran over and barked at him. Dusty's
foot lashed out. Tom's jaw dropped open
in shock as the little Chihuahua narrowly

avoided being kicked. Chilli yelped, and dashed out of the way.

Zuma scooped him into her arms. "What did you do that for?" she shouted angrily at Dusty.

The outlaw stopped. He turned to look at her. "I hate dogs," he snarled. "A dingo bit me when I was a boy, and I can't stand the sight of them now."

"But Chilli wouldn't hurt anyone," said Zuma, holding up the Chihuahua. "Look at him. He's just small and friendly."

"I don't trust any dog," said Dusty. For a second he looked scared. Then the look of fear disappeared, and with a fresh scowl he turned and stomped away.

Zuma gave Chilli a hug and returned to the dance. Tom found a chair and sat down to watch. Beside him, a grizzled old man strummed a guitar.

Leaning over, Tom asked, "I don't understand how Ben Hall can be a thief but everyone still likes him so much."

The old man gave Tom a toothless grin. "He's a thief all right," he said in a wheezing voice. "But he shares what he steals."

Seeing Tom's puzzled face, the old man slapped his guitar with a laugh. "You're a stranger round here, aren't you?" he asked.

Tom nodded.

"Well, stranger," the old man continued, "maybe you don't understand life in the outback. There's a few rich folk who own all the land. The rest of us are as poor as dirt. It ain't right and it ain't fair! The law says that bushrangers are criminals, but Ben Hall takes from the rich and looks out for the common folk. That makes him all right, if you ask me."

Before Tom could ask any more questions,
the old man turned back to his guitar and
began to sing:

"They said Captain Thunderbolt took a horse;
The judge sent him to Cockatoo Island, of course.
There he works under the blazing sun,
Breaking rocks for what he's done.
Ten years' hard labour – now that's a crime,
Ten years of suffering heat, dust and grime."

Behind Tom, someone began clapping
along to the old man's song. It was Ben Hall.
Up close, the outlaw was a frightening sight.
His face had been tanned to the colour of
leather. His clothes were dusty. A gun hung
from his hip. Nonetheless, the riddle had
made it clear that 'Brave' Ben Hall would
lead him and Zuma to the golden coin.

Tom gulped. He had to talk to the outlaw. "Excuse me," he said politely. "Who's Captain Thunderbolt?"

Ben Hall looked down at him. "Why, the captain is the 'gentleman bushranger'," he said. "His real name is Frederick Ward. Twice the police tried to send him to prison for petty crimes. Both times he was set free. In the end, they said he'd stolen a horse. The judge locked him away on Cockatoo Island for ten years."

As Ben finished, a woman caught him by the arm. Together, they whirled away into the dance. A second later, Zuma spun past.

Tom grabbed her. "Hey," he said. "We're supposed to be looking for Tlaloc's coin, remember?"

"But I'm having fun," Zuma replied. She crossed her arms. A stubborn look appeared on her face. "It's the first party I've ever been to. When you're an Aztec slave, life is all work, work, work… and human sacrifice. Slaves are *never* allowed to have a good time."

"Yes, but if we don't find the coin, you'll *always* be a slave," Tom told her firmly. "Come on, we've got work to do. I want to take a closer look at Ben Hall's bag of loot. Maybe the coin is mixed up with the gold and jewels in there."

"Good idea," said Zuma. Her face brightened at the thought that the third gold coin might be close by. She pointed across the room. "Dusty Moore went that way."

They opened a door to a small, private dining room. Inside, Dusty Moore looked up and glared at them. Spread across the table in front of him was a heap of gold and jewels and piles of money. In one of Dusty's hands

was a leather bag. In the other was a fistful of
jewellery.

Tom and Zuma gasped at the same time.
Hanging from Dusty's fingers was a necklace.
Hanging from the end of the necklace was
a gold Aztec coin stamped with an image of
the sun.

"The third coin!" whispered Zuma, staring at it.

Dusty Moore ignored her. "What are you doing here?" he growled, dropping the coin into his bag.

"I could ask you the same question," Tom replied, staring at the bag. It was already half full of Ben Hall's loot.

A sneer crossed the outlaw's face. "Brave Ben Hall might want to waste his swag throwing parties for the poor, but not me," he spat. "I'm a *real* outlaw. The poor can stay poor. I don't care. This swag will make me rich for life."

"You'll never get away with this!" Zuma hissed. "I'm going to get Ben Hall." She began backing away, opening her mouth to call for help.

Dusty Moore pulled out a gun. He

pointed it at Zuma's face. "Say one word, missy, and both you and your friend are dead."

CHAPTER 4

QUICK GETAWAY

Tom and Zuma stared down the barrel of Dusty Moore's gun. The outlaw tipped the rest of the loot into his bag and backed towards an open door that led on to the street.

"Come here and keep your mouths shut," he said, beckoning them outside. "I don't want you hollering for help as soon as I'm gone."

Tom and Zuma had no choice but to follow Dusty out into the empty street. The gang's horses were tied to a railing outside

the hotel. Dusty chose the biggest – a black
stallion. He kept his gun on Tom and Zuma
while he untied the rest, yelling and slapping
their hindquarters. Whinnying, the horses
galloped off down the street.

Dusty climbed into the saddle of the black
stallion. With a cry of triumph, he kicked the
horse's flanks. A trail of dirt flew up into the
air as the outlaw sped away.

"How are we going to catch up with him?" whispered Zuma through gritted teeth.

"I don't know, but we have to try," Tom replied. "Come on! We have to tell Ben Hall. He's the only person who can help us get the coin back."

Together, Tom and Zuma raced back inside the hotel. Ben Hall was still whirling his partner round the floor. They pushed their way through the crowd towards him.

"Mr Hall!" Zuma shouted over the noise. "We need to speak to you. It's important!"

Ben frowned at her. "Not now, little lady. Can't you see I'm busy," he said, dancing away from her.

"Dusty Moore's stolen your loot!" Tom yelled.

"What?!" Ben Hall immediately stopped

dancing. He spun round to face Tom and Zuma.

"It's true," shouted Zuma. "We caught him red-handed. He's stolen a horse and gone!"

Ben Hall's tanned face grew even darker with anger. "That low-down dingo's backside!" he bellowed. "No one cheats Brave Ben Hall out of his swag. I'll track him down and make him pay." He turned to his men, who had gathered round the piano. "Stay here and keep the party going," he told them. "I'll be back tomorrow!"

The bushranger stomped towards the hotel's main door.

"Wait!" Tom shouted after him. "We'll come with you."

Ben stopped and looked back. "A couple

of kids like you will just slow me down," he said.

"That's what *you* think," Zuma replied, crossing her arms. "You may be brave, but *I've* escaped from being a human sacrifice. That's not easy when you're carrying a small dog and you've got twenty priests hot on your heels."

"I've fought a ninja," said Tom. "That was pretty scary, but we took care of him."

"And Chilli's the bravest dog around," added Zuma.

Chilli barked and puffed out his chest.

Ben Hall stared at them both in confusion. "What in the blazes are you talking about?" he began. Shaking his head, he continued, "No, I don't have time for you to tell me. Come along if you want. I'm thankful you raised the alarm and I suppose there's a vacancy in the gang, now that double-crossing Dusty has disappeared. I'm warning you, though – if you fall behind, I'm not waiting for you to catch up."

"Don't worry about us," said Tom. "I promise we won't slow you down."

Zuma dashed past him at top speed. "Just watch me go!" she shouted. Sprinting through the door, she took off up the road. Chilli was close behind, yapping with excitement.

Ben Hall followed at a run. "Hold up," he called after her. "It'll be quicker if we ride."

"But Dusty let all your horses loose," Tom explained.

Ben turned to him and winked. "That's the great thing about being a bushranger," he said. "If you lose your horse, you can always steal another. Follow me."

"Wait a minute," said Tom. "We might be

desperate, but we're not stealing. If it wasn't
for us, you wouldn't even know your loot
was missing."

Ben Hall thought for a moment.

"Yeah," Zuma continued, "we're not as
bad as Dusty Moore!"

That seemed to do the trick. "OK, kids,"
said Ben Hall. "You wait here."

A couple of minutes later, Tom and Zuma
watched as the bushranger appeared leading
three sleek horses behind him. "I found
these tied up by the police station," he said.
"They're racehorses, so we'll catch up with
Dusty in no time. And don't worry, I gave
that policeman we locked up in the cells a
fair price for them."

Tom and Zuma grinned.

"There's no time to find saddles, though,"
said Ben. "If you want to come with me,

you'll have to ride bareback."

"I'm sure there's nothing to it," Zuma said. Tucking Chilli under one arm, she climbed up the fence and vaulted on to the back of a brown horse with a white stripe on its forehead. It reared beneath her, hooves pawing at the air. The little Chihuahua safely in her lap, Zuma clung on to the horse's mane. The horse calmed down. "There," she said with a grin. "It's as easy as falling off a pyramid."

"Or as easy as falling off a galloping horse," Tom muttered to himself. He climbed on to his racehorse nervously. He had ridden many horses during his time-travel adventures, and Zuma had learned how to ride in the Wild West and when they visited Medieval Japan. Even so, neither of them had ever tried it without a saddle.

"It takes a while to get used to. Just relax and keep looking where you want to go," Ben Hall told them. "If you look down at the horse, you'll lose your balance."

"Dusty went that way," said Zuma. She pointed down the road.

"Come on then," Ben said back. "I'm going to pull that good-for-nothing's ears off when we catch him."

At that moment, a shot rang out. The fence post next to Tom exploded in a shower of splinters. Zuma gasped at the loud *crack*. Chilli buried his face in her lap with a yelp.

Ben's head spun round. "Behind you!" he yelled, pointing down the road. "Police – five of them! They must have heard that me and the gang were heading this way."

Clouds of dust were rising up from the ground as more shots bit into the dirt. Tom was amazed to see that Ben Hall was laughing. The bushranger was obviously no stranger to danger.

Gripping his horse's mane, Ben yelled, "Yah!" The racehorse reared and galloped away like a rocket.

"YAH!" yelled Zuma and Tom together.

Tom's horse leaped forward with an excited snort. Zuma's was right beside him. Bullets buzzed through the air like angry insects. Tom leaned forward over his horse's neck. His heart beat like a drum. Around him, the craggy landscape whizzed by at breathtaking speed. Riding bareback was nothing like riding with a saddle. It was much more difficult keeping his balance, but it was almost like Tom was part of the horse. He could feel its muscles moving powerfully beneath him.

Holding on to the mane for dear life, Tom tried not to think about what would happen if the police caught up with them. They'd only been in Australia for a couple of hours, but already he and Zuma had managed to get involved with an outlaw gang and now they were being shot at by the police!

Tlaloc's quests *were* getting more dangerous. If they were caught now they'd probably end up in prison on Cockatoo Island with Captain Thunderbolt!

CHAPTER 5
ON THE RUN

Tom's horse pounded the hard ground with its hooves as it put on a fresh burst of speed. Beside him, Zuma's face was determined as she clung on to her horse's mane. Behind them, the police shouted and fired more shots. Tom felt a tugging at his shirt. Looking down he saw a hole that hadn't been there a moment before. One of the bullets had torn through the material!

"Yah!" he shouted into the horse's ear.

"Gee up!" Despite the danger, he felt a wild surge of excitement. Ben Hall had been right – the horses were amazing. Tom may have ridden horses before, but none of them had been as swift as a racehorse.

"That way!" Zuma shouted. Tom's eyes followed her pointing finger. Ahead of them Ben had swerved off the road. Now he was galloping up a small track towards the distant hills. Tom tugged on his horse's mane and risked a glance back. Through a thick cloud of dust, he could see the police had fallen behind. Their horses couldn't keep up.

Tom and Zuma continued to urge on their horses, keeping their eyes fixed on Ben Hall. The outlaw had turned his horse again and was riding in the direction of a narrow valley.

"Look out!" Tom cried a moment later. Ahead of them was a fence. Barbed wire was strung between high posts. The horses were galloping too fast to stop. Tom clenched his teeth, certain that they were going to be cut to ribbons.

Ben didn't even try to avoid it. "Jump!" he yelled back. His horse leaped, clearing the fence easily.

Tom's heart pounded. The fence was coming up fast. He squeezed his eyes closed. The horse's muscles tensed beneath him. For a second Tom felt like he was flying. He gripped the mane until his knuckles went white.

With a jolt, the horse landed on the other side. Tom's eyes snapped open. He'd made it! A moment later, he heard Zuma whooping with joy as her own horse cleared the deadly fence.

"We're not safe yet," Ben Hall called back.

"Keep going!"

Eventually, the shots behind them stopped. Tom glanced round again. The police were nowhere to be seen. Ahead, the outlaw was finally slowing down. He stopped beneath a tree, and slipped off his horse's back.

Tom and Zuma brought their own horses to a halt beside him. Both of their animals were panting, their coats covered in sweat.

Ben crouched down in the middle of the dry track until his nose was almost pressed into the dirt. "Dusty came this way," he said, pointing to the ground.

Leaning over, Tom stared. He couldn't see anything but cracked mud.

"I thought he'd get off the main road as soon as he could, and this is the only track round here," Ben told him. "Now a horse is a heavy beast, especially when it's carrying a man. Even when the ground's as hard as iron it'll leave tracks if you look hard enough."

"I see them," said Zuma excitedly. Her sharp eyes had easily picked out the faint hoof marks in the ground.

Ben nodded. "These are fresh – it's got to be Dusty. He's heading east. Probably making for the coast so he can sell the jewels in the city."

"Our horses are faster than his. He can't be far ahead," said Tom.

"And the police won't be far behind," Zuma added.

Ben nodded. "If we can keep ahead of the police, we'll catch him before sundown. Then we'll find somewhere to hide out overnight." The outlaw swung himself on to his horse's back.

The horses were tired, but Ben kept up

a fast pace until they came to a river. The outlaw stopped his horse and looked round at Tom and Zuma. "It's fast, but shallow," he said. "The horses will get us across all right and we can pick up Dusty's trail on the other side. You two go first. I'm going to brush away our tracks and make it harder for the police to follow us."

As the bushranger started scuffing out their tracks in the dirt Tom and Zuma rode their snorting horses into the water. The horses were able to pick their way across easily. Even so, by the time they were halfway over, the river was up to their knees. Zuma leaned out. Cupping her hand, she drank the cool water. Tom drank some too and then kicked out with his foot, splashing her.

"Hey!" she said. "What was that for?"

"You said you wanted to stand underneath

a waterfall," Tom reminded her. "This is the next best thing."

Zuma's grin faded from her face. She twisted round in her saddle. "What was that?" she asked.

"What was what?" chuckled Tom.

"*That!*" shouted Zuma.

This time Tom heard the long rumble of thunder that echoed through the hills.

Above them, black clouds suddenly swirled across the sky. As it grew darker, Tom felt cold raindrops on his face. A second later they were caught in a torrential rainstorm.

Rearing up in fright, the racehorses threw Tom and Zuma off their backs and into the river.

At once Tom felt the strong current threatening to drag him downstream. He grabbed hold of Zuma's sleeve, and together they struggled to their feet. Wiping the water from his eyes, Tom saw their horses frantically charging back to the bank. He and Zuma were alone in the river.

"It's Tlaloc!" Zuma yelled. "We have to get out of here!"

Tom didn't need telling twice. But before he could wade towards dry land, Tlaloc's face loomed large in the sky above them, roaring with laughter. "Too late!" he boomed.

The gushing sound of the river became louder and louder. Zuma gasped. Eyes wide, Tom looked round. Tlaloc had conjured up a foaming wall of water and it was heading straight towards them.

"It's a flash flood!" bellowed Ben Hall from the bank. "Move it! NOW!"

CHAPTER 6
SNAKE IN THE GRASS

The water smashed into Tom like a hammer. He heard Zuma cry out, but there was nothing he could do to help. Tom managed to take one gulp of air before he was dragged under the surface and swept downstream. The rushing water rolled and tossed him about as if he were a twig.

Just when he thought his lungs were going to burst, Tom's head bobbed to the surface. Gulping for air, he looked round desperately.

Luckily, he saw he was close to the riverbank. Tom summoned every ounce of strength he had and began to swim towards dry land. At last, exhausted, he grabbed hold of a dangling tree branch and pulled himself on to the bank.

The rain had stopped and the sky was clear blue again. But the river was still swollen with water, churning and rolling. Tom frantically scanned the surface for Zuma and Chilli, but there was no sign of either of them. His heart sank. Had they been swept away by the flash flood?

"Tom!" he heard a familiar voice cry out. "Over here!"

Turning round, Tom let out a huge sigh of relief. Zuma was sitting further up the bank, wringing water from her sodden clothes. Chilli was sitting in a puddle beside her. As Tom walked over, the Chihuahua stood up and shook himself dry, spraying the air with water droplets.

"That was close," said Zuma.

"Too close," said Tom, puffing out his cheeks. "Tlaloc nearly ended our quest

once and for all."

"Hey, kids!" a voice yelled.

They looked up to see Ben Hall waving
from the opposite bank. He was still sitting

on his horse, shielding his eyes against the sun as he looked over towards Tom and Zuma.

"Glad you're OK!" Ben yelled. "I thought you two were goners for a moment there. I've never seen a flood like that!"

Tom cupped his hands round his mouth. "Can you get across?"

"Not a chance," the outlaw shouted back. "The water's too deep now. It'll be hours before the river's safe to cross."

"So what shall we do?" said Zuma, shaking the water out of her hair.

"You two will have to go after Dusty and the loot on your own," Ben called back. "I can't stay here – the police are still on our trail. I'll lead them off in another direction. Head east and keep your eyes peeled. I'll catch up with you as soon as I can." He held up his bushranger knife in a final salute, before turning his horse and galloping away.

"We'd better go before we're spotted," said Tom.

"Good idea," said Zuma. "I've had enough of rivers for one adventure."

Following Ben's directions, they went east, scanning the ground for tracks of Dusty's horse. It didn't take long for their clothes to dry in the blazing sun. Soon they were sweltering in the heat again.

Tom's hat had been washed away in the flood and his forehead was damp with sweat. Even so, he couldn't help looking about in wonder. The Australian outback was hot and dry, but amazing. Among the craggy rocks were thick bushes and tall trees. Bright flowers grew in their shade.

"Why are you laughing?" Zuma asked suddenly.

Tom blinked. "What? I wasn't laughing."

"I heard you," Zuma replied. "We're on our own and there's no one else for miles. There's nothing funny about it."

"I didn't—" Tom started to say, only to be interrupted by the sound of loud laughter.

He and Zuma both looked up. In the branches above their heads was a brown bird with a sharp beak. "It must be a kookaburra," said Tom.

"I saw a picture of one in a book about Australia."

"Well, I wish it wouldn't do that," said Zuma. "It sounds like it's making fun of us."

"It's just singing," Tom told her. "It's not really laughing."

"Sorry," said Zuma. "I don't mean to
be grumpy, but I'm so hot and thirsty. I'd
almost be glad to see Tlaloc again. At least it
would mean some rain."

"Wait!" cried Tom. "Look!"

He pointed excitedly at the ground in front
of them. As if by magic, a trail of hoofprints

had suddenly appeared in the dirt, leading off into the distance.

"Do you think that's Dusty's horse?" asked Zuma.

"Who else's could it be?" said Tom. "Come on!"

They carried on with new energy, following the trail of prints along the ground. As they walked, Tom wondered what would happen once they caught up with the bushranger. After all, they were alone and Dusty was armed. They would have to use their brains and their cunning if they were going to get Tlaloc's coin and complete this latest quest.

The tracks continued through a narrow path between two large rocks. Tom and Zuma were grateful for the shade as they passed through the rocks, and Chilli yapped his approval. They came out on the other side to find sunshine glittering on the surface of a small lake surrounded by reeds. They searched round the lake, but the tracks seem to have disappeared. If they couldn't pick up the trail again they would never find the coin.

"Oh, well," said Zuma, forcing a smile. "At least we can have a drink at last!" Zuma turned and ran towards the water.

Tom quickly caught up with her, with Chilli nipping excitedly at his heels. A few seconds later, they were crouched in the shallows beside a wooden sign. On it someone had scratched the words 'The Thirsty Billabong'.

"We found it! This must be the billabong from the riddle," cried Tom.

Cupping her hands, Zuma drank deeply. "Oh, that's good," she gasped between gulps. "My throat was starting to feel like a desert."

Zuma didn't get any further. Darting forward, Tom grabbed her arm. She squealed as he yanked her out of the water.

"What did you do that for?" she spluttered.

Tom said nothing. He just pointed. A V-shaped ripple was heading through the water towards them. Bubbling up out of the murky deep, a snake emerged. Six feet long and dark brown with lighter diamond patches along its back, it slithered up on to the grassy bank. Hissing angrily at them, it opened its mouth to show fangs dripping with venom.

CHAPTER 7
WALKABOUT

Tom and Zuma froze. The snake reared its head, a long forked tongue flicking in and out between its sharp fangs.

"Let's back away," Tom said quietly to Zuma. "And don't make a sound."

Zuma glanced over her shoulder. "There's a tree about a metre behind us," she whispered. "When I say 'go', jump behind it."

Tom nodded.

"Three… two… one… go!"

Both of them took a big step backwards and then jumped behind the tree. Tom peered round its wide trunk. The snake glared at him, hissing, then slithered beneath a rotten log.

"Is it safe to make a run for it?" Zuma whispered.

"I don't know," Tom replied. "It's still there."

"Just our luck," Zuma groaned. "The only water for miles and it's infested with killer snakes."

"Hello," said a cheerful voice behind them. "What are you two looking at?"

Tom almost jumped out of his skin. Turning quickly, he saw the voice belonged to a dark-skinned teenage boy. Round his waist he wore a simple white cloth. His body was covered with faded white paint. His mouth was open in a wide and friendly grin.

"I'm Monti," said the boy. "What are you doing way out here?"

"Shh!" Zuma hissed. "There's a huge, terrifying snake over by that log. It's got long fangs dripping with poison."

"Sounds pretty scary," said Monti. "I'd better take a look." He peered across at the rotten log. When he spotted the snake, Monti burst out laughing. "It's just a Copperhead," he said. "There's enough venom in those fangs to kill you, all right, but it's a really shy snake. It's probably more scared of you than you are of it."

Tom breathed a sigh of relief. "Thanks, Monti. This is our first time in the outback, and we're a long way from home. I'm Tom, and this is Zuma."

"No problem," said the teenager. "Nice to meet you. Hot, isn't it? I've been wandering about out here for two months now."

"Why?" asked Tom. "Don't you have a home?"

"Sure," Monti replied. "But I'm on Walkabout. My people have been living out here for thousands of years. When a boy reaches thirteen, he goes into the outback alone. He can be out there for months, proving that he can take care of himself. When he comes home, he's a man."

"But how do you survive?" Tom asked.

Monti laughed again. "There's plenty of food if you know where to look for it," he said. "And I have this for hunting." He pulled out a bent piece of carved wood painted with strange symbols from the rope round his waist.

"A boomerang!" said Tom. "I've heard of them. Do they really return when you throw them?"

In answer, Monti pulled back his arm and hurled the boomerang. It whirled round in a giant circle. A couple of seconds later he caught it expertly. "Want to try?" he asked.

"Yes!" said Tom and Zuma at the same time.

Tom couldn't get the hang of the boomerang. After a few tries, he was tired of searching through bushes trying to find it. Zuma, however, was a natural. Soon, she was hurling it into the sky and catching it easily when it returned to her.

"Hey, you're good," said Monti.

"Thanks, Monti," beamed Zuma. She gave Tom a sideways look. "See? Told you I had loads of talents."

"You still haven't told me what the two of you are doing out here," Monti said.

"We're looking for an outlaw called Dusty Moore. He's stolen something that belongs to Zuma," said Tom. "We followed his tracks to the billabong, but now we don't know which way he went."

"Really?" said Monti. "I nearly got trampled by a fellow on a big black horse a couple of hours ago. The man riding it was wearing a straw hat and a red shirt."

"That's him!" gasped Tom. "That's Dusty!"

"Can you show us which way he went?" asked Zuma.

"I can do better than that," said Monti. "I'll take you straight to him."

After filling his billycan with water, Monti led Tom and Zuma east, along the path of a dried-up creek. After a couple of minutes the boy crouched down. He pointed out a trail of scuffed marks in the dirt. "There you go," he said. "It shows a man on horseback passed by recently – and he was going fast too."

"The tracks look quite faint," Tom said dubiously. "Can you follow them?"

Monti grinned. "With my eyes closed," he said.

Following Monti and Chilli, Tom and Zuma set off again. Their gloominess had disappeared. They were on the right path to finding Dusty and the golden coin.

"Oh, look at that," said Zuma after a while. She was pointing up into a tree. A small fluffy creature with big ears and a black nose clung to a branch, slowly eating a pawful of leaves. "What a cute animal."

"It's a koala," Monti told her. "There are loads of different animals out here. Can you see the wallaby over by that rock?"

Tom and Zuma's eyes followed his pointing finger. "It's like a tiny kangaroo," said Tom.

Hearing his voice, the wallaby looked up and bounced away.

"Not all the creatures are harmless," Monti said. "There are poisonous snakes, and spiders like this funnel web." He stopped by a shaded rock and pointed at an ugly, ten-centimetre black spider that had built its web into a crack.

"Yikes," said Zuma, backing away. "I was going to walk right past it."

"You've already walked past a dozen of them," grinned Monti.

Tom looked round nervously. Suddenly, the Australian outback seemed full of danger.

"And that's an emu," Monti continued, pointing out a two-metre tall bird that was running across the horizon. He pulled out his boomerang. "They taste really good, but it takes a while to cook them."

"We're in a bit of a hurry," said Tom.

"I *am* hungry, though," Zuma added. "We haven't eaten all day."

Monti looked up at a gnarled tree with

silvery-grey bark. "Luckily, this is a River
Red Gum tree," he said. "So I can get you a
snack right now."

Picking up a rock, he dug down into

the earth between the tree's roots. A few moments later, he held out a handful of wriggling white worms.

Monti popped one in his mouth and began chewing. With his mouth full he said, "Witchetty grubs are delicious. Try one."

"Ugh! No thanks," said Tom.

But Zuma didn't have to be asked twice. Taking a grub from Monti's hand, she munched it quickly. "Mmm, tastes good," she said.

Tom's nose wrinkled. The grubs looked disgusting. Even so, he was starving and didn't know when he'd next eat. And he didn't want Monti to think he was squeamish – especially when Zuma had been so fast to eat one. He picked up a grub from Monti's palm and popped it in his mouth. He tried not to think about it being a wriggling insect

97

as he bit down. The grub burst, filling Tom's mouth with warm goo. He forced himself to chew and swallow. Once the grub had stopped wriggling, it tasted surprisingly sweet.

Monti grinned. "You're a *real* outback bushman now," he said, holding out his hand. "Want another?"

When they had eaten all the grubs they could stomach, Monti continued on down the trail.

An hour later they stood on a low hill looking across a vast stretch of blue. They had reached the wide Parramatta River. Tom and Zuma hurried down until they were standing on the grassy bank. Tom was grateful for the cool breeze coming off the water.

In the middle of the river was a large strip of land. "That's Cockatoo Island," Monti told them.

"The prison where they send bushrangers?"
Tom said.

"That's right—" Monti began.

He was interrupted by a cry and a
tremendous splash.

"There's a man out there!" Zuma shouted.

Sure enough, a large man was thrashing through the water. Tom's jaw dropped. He had jumped off the island into the river. "He must be escaping from the prison!" he shouted.

"He's mad," Monti cried. "These waters are swarming with bull sharks. Look!" He pointed down the river.

Tom's heart sank as he saw the black triangle of a shark's fin poking out of the water. Picking up speed, the bull shark began streaking through the water towards the prisoner!

CHAPTER 8
JAILBREAK!

"He'll be eaten alive!" yelled Tom. "We have to help." Without stopping to think, he dashed down the bank and waded out into the river. He had to fight the strong current to stay upright.

"Stop, Tom!" shouted Zuma behind him. "The shark will get you too!"

Tom splashed to a halt. Zuma was right. If he swam out to help the prisoner, he'd be eaten as well. "What else can we do?" he yelled over his shoulder.

"Let me have a go," said Zuma. She grabbed the boomerang from Monti's rope belt. Running forward a few steps, she hurled it with all her strength.

Tom held his breath as it whirled across the water.

Thunk! the boomerang clipped the shark's fin. Tom leaped up, punching the air. He whooped as the bull shark changed direction and swam away from the prisoner.

Zuma reached up and caught the returning boomerang. "It's lucky I'm so talented," she said.

Tom didn't stop to reply. Wading further out, he reached the exhausted prisoner and helped him out of the water.

For a while, the man lay panting on the bank. Tom and Zuma looked him up and down. Like Ben Hall he had a bushy beard, but his hair was longer. His clothes were old and tattered, his feet bare.

Eventually, he opened his eyes. He looked from Tom's worried face to Zuma's. "Good day. My thanks to you," he said in a deep voice. "Frederick Wordsworth Ward, at your service."

Tom frowned. He was sure he had heard the name before. Suddenly, he remembered. "Frederick Ward!" he said. "Ben Hall told me about you. You're Captain Thunderbolt! You stole a horse and got sentenced to ten years in prison!"

Chuckling, Frederick Ward sat up. "That's me all right," he said. "And if it wasn't for you two, Captain Thunderbolt would be inside that shark's belly by now." He stopped. His voice became serious as he continued. "You've made yourself a mate for life. If there's anything I can do in return, just say the word. What are your names?"

"I'm Tom," Tom told him.

"And I'm Zuma," added Zuma. "It was me who hit the shark with the boomerang. Just in case you were wondering."

Monti joined them. He was shaking his head sadly. "I've lost the tracks of that fellow you're after," he said. "They stop at the bank. I think he might have waded down the river."

Tom looked thoughtfully at Captain Thunderbolt. "Maybe *you* could help us," he said. "We're looking for an outlaw named Dusty Moore. He stole Ben Hall's loot. There's a gold coin in it that belongs to Zuma. It's really important that we find it."

"We've tracked him this far," Zuma continued. "Do you know where he might be going?"

"Dusty Moore?" Captain Thunderbolt

nodded. "That's a name I haven't heard in a while. We used to ride with the same gang before he joined up with Ben Hall. Dusty was a nasty piece of work – mean, and dangerous too."

"He hasn't changed much," said Zuma glumly.

"Back when I knew him Dusty used to have a hideout not far from here. I don't think he's used it in years," said the captain. "But if he's on the run from Ben Hall it would be the perfect place to lie low." He got to his feet. "I can probably still find it. But a couple of kids like you shouldn't be meddling with someone like that all on your own. Whatever happens, you'll have Captain Thunderbolt right at your side."

Monti grinned. "Well, it looks like you two don't need my help any more," he told

Tom and Zuma. "And I've got a Walkabout to finish."

Zuma gave him a hug. "Thanks for your help, Monti," she said.

"We'd never have come this far without you," Tom added. He grinned. "And I'd never have tasted witchetty grubs, either."

Monti laughed. "Good luck, both of you. Keep a lookout for terrifying snakes." With a final wave, he walked back into the bush.

When Monti was out of sight, Captain Thunderbolt shaded his eyes from the sun and looked along the river. "As I remember, Dusty's place is this way," he said, striding along the bank. Tom and Zuma ran after him.

"I bet you're glad to get off Cockatoo Island, Captain," Tom said. "It must have been pretty bad to make you risk swimming through a shark-infested river."

"You can say that again," the outlaw replied. "It's no place for a man who loves the outback as much as I do. Believe me, I'm never going back."

They followed the path of the river for about another hour before the outlaw came to a halt and pointed to a shack nestled away in the trees. "This is the place."

Panting, Chilli quickly found some shade and lay down.

"Poor doggie," said Zuma. "You've walked a long way and you've only got little legs."

In reply, Chilli put his head on his front paws and barked quietly.

"Zuma!" whispered Tom urgently. "We're *supposed* to be creeping up on a dangerous outlaw, remember?"

"Of course I remember," Zuma whispered

back. She turned to look at Dusty Moore's hideout. The small rickety shack looked like it had been built from pieces of driftwood. Set back from the riverbank, it was almost completely hidden by scrubby trees and bushes.

"Looks like he's at home," said Captain Thunderbolt in a deep growl. "There's a black stallion tied up outside."

"The same one he took from outside the hotel," said Tom. He turned to Zuma, eyes wide with excitement.

She returned his look. "We're *so* close," she whispered. "Tlaloc's coin must be inside. How can we get it without Dusty trying to stop us?"

"Get down! Out of sight, you two," hissed Captain Thunderbolt suddenly. He ducked behind a bush.

Zuma grabbed Tom and pulled him
behind a tree trunk as the shack's door
opened. It was Dusty Moore, still dressed in

the same straw hat and red shirt. He peered round the door and looked out, checking the coast was clear. Then he walked off with an empty bucket in his hand, whistling a jaunty tune. A moment later, he disappeared behind a large rock.

"There's a creek round the corner," Captain Thunderbolt said. "He's gone for water. That gives us a few minutes to find your swag."

"Let's go," said Zuma. In a flash, she streaked out from behind the tree and dashed towards the hut. Tom and the captain followed.

A second later, they were all standing inside Dusty's secret hideout. "There aren't many hiding places here," said Tom. His voice sounded doubtful. The small hut contained only a rough wooden bed covered

with a single blanket, a table, one chair and
a chest.

"Ben Hall's loot's got to be here
somewhere," whispered Captain
Thunderbolt. "You look under the bed,
I'll check the chest." The outlaw flung
open the lid of the chest and peered inside.
Meanwhile, Tom lifted up the bed so Zuma
could crouch down and look underneath it.
"Nothing here," she reported. She stood up
and frowned.

Dropping the bed, Tom flung back the
blanket. "Or here," he muttered.

Captain Thunderbolt was tossing clothes,
lengths of rope and a few tools out of the
chest, but there was no sign of any treasure.

"Sorry, kids," he groaned. "Wherever
Dusty's hidden the swag, it's not here."

A shadow fell across the floor. Tom,

Zuma and Captain Thunderbolt all looked round at the same moment.

Straight down the barrel of Dusty Hall's gun.

CHAPTER 9

HIDEOUT HIGH JINKS

"Idiots," Dusty sneered. "Don't you think I keep a watch of my own hideout? I saw you coming, so I set a little trap. And you walked straight into it. *Idiots*," he repeated the word with a curl of his lip.

Captain Thunderbolt scowled. "If anyone's an idiot it's you, Dusty. You give bushrangers a bad name."

Dusty chuckled nastily. "Bushranger? It's a nice way of saying 'thief', Captain. We're all thieves. Only I don't dress it up in fancy words."

"Some of us only steal from folk that can afford it and share our loot with the folk that need it," Captain Thunderbolt growled.

"Too bad I've outwitted you then," Dusty replied. "Just like I outwitted Brave Ben Hall. I guess that makes me the greatest bushranger in the land!"

"You didn't outwit anybody," retorted Zuma. "You waited until Ben Hall's back was turned and then you ran away before he could catch up with you. You're nothing more than a big scaredy-cat."

"Shut your mouth!" Dusty spat on the floor, then he turned his pistol on Tom and Zuma. "I should have shot you two meddling kids when I had the chance," he said. "It would've saved me all this fuss. I guess I'll just have to do it now."

Dusty's finger tightened on the trigger. A shiver of fear went down Tom's back. Then, from the corner of his eye he saw a small movement through the open door – Chilli!

In a flash, Tom remembered that Dusty hated dogs. He'd looked terrified when Zuma had held Chilli up to him back at the hotel. "Hey, Dusty," he shouted, pointing behind the outlaw. "Is that a dingo out there?"

Chilli seemed to understand. As Tom said the word 'dingo', the little Chihuahua snarled his deepest snarl and jumped at Dusty Moore. Clinging to the outlaw's leg, he sunk his teeth into his calf.

"Get it off me!" Dusty shrieked. Flapping

his arms, he screamed and spun round the
room. "Get it off! GET IT OFF!"

The gun flew across the tiny shack and landed at Captain Thunderbolt's feet. In one movement, he crouched and picked it up. Pointing the gun at the ceiling, he fired a single shot through the roof. Clicking the hammer back, he pointed the gun at Dusty. "Hands to the sky," he growled.

Instantly, the outlaw stopped. His face paled. Slowly, he put his hands in the air.

Zuma darted forward. Scooping Chilli off Dusty's leg, she held the little dog tightly and scratched his ears. Chilli barked happily. "He's usually very friendly," she told the outlaw. "But he doesn't seem to like you very much. I wonder why?"

Dusty Moore glared at her and cursed.

"Watch your mouth," said Captain Thunderbolt. He waved the gun towards the chair. "Take a seat, Dusty. There are plenty of folk who'll happily collect the reward for handing you in. Once I've tied you up I'll let them know where to find you."

"I can tie him up, Captain," said Tom. He picked up a coiled rope and wound it round the snarling Dusty. Tom had learned to tie a proper knot on a pirate ship during a previous time-travel adventure, and he made sure Dusty couldn't escape.

"Good work there, kid," said Captain Thunderbolt. He grinned at Dusty. "Say hello to all the fellows back on Cockatoo Island for me, won't you, Dusty! And I wouldn't try swimming off if I were you. There are a whole lot of sharks in the river, and you might not be as lucky as I was."

Although the captain was grinning from ear to ear, he noticed that Tom and Zuma weren't looking quite so happy. "Why are you two so glum?" he asked.

"We might have found Dusty, but we still haven't found that coin," replied Zuma.

"And you never will," Dusty sneered. "I won't tell you where I've hidden it."

"I said keep your mouth shut, Dusty, or I'll gag you as well." Captain Thunderbolt stroked his beard thoughtfully. "He might have buried it outside," he said. "Or maybe we should search his horse's saddlebags."

"What about the riddle, Tom?" Zuma suggested. "Didn't it say something about the swag being under a tree?"

Tom nodded. "A cabbage tree," he

said. "But I've no idea what it meant. I've never even heard of a cabbage tree and I don't know what one looks like…"

His voice trailed off. Captain Thunderbolt was roaring with laughter. Red-faced, he slapped his knee.

"What's so funny?" said Zuma.

"Don't you kids know what a cabbage tree is?" the captain spluttered. "I thought *everyone* knew that."

Tom and Zuma stared at him. "Um… we're travellers," said Tom. "We're not from round here."

"So what *is* a cabbage tree?" asked Zuma.

"It's a hat," chuckled Captain Thunderbolt. "A big hat. Everyone wears them."

"A hat like this one?" asked Zuma.

Reaching out, she swept the hat off Dusty
Moore's head. Underneath, a small leather
pouch was attached to the inside brim
of the hat. The pouch jingled when she
picked it up.

"*Exactly* like that one," Captain Thunderbolt smiled.

Zuma emptied the pouch on to the table. Money and jewellery spilled out across the wooden surface. In the centre was a golden chain with a glittering Aztec coin attached to it.

"Tlaloc's coin!" she shouted in delight. The slave girl picked up the chain and dangled it from her fingers. "We did it, Tom. We beat Tlaloc *again*!"

Tom beamed happily. Turning to Captain Thunderbolt, he said, "Thanks for all your help. We have to go now."

"But what about the rest of the swag?" asked the captain.

"It belongs to Ben Hall," said Tom. "At least, it was Ben Hall that stole it. Give it to him. Tell him to throw the biggest party

Australia has ever seen."

"Now that's a great idea," laughed Captain Thunderbolt.

"Come on, Tom," Zuma interrupted. "Let's get back before Tlaloc springs another nasty surprise on us." Holding Chilli close, she touched the coin. Tom did the same.

A blanket of shimmering mist fell on them. Within a second, Tom could see nothing but twinkling lights in the strange fog.

"Goodbye, Captain Thunderbolt!" he heard Zuma call out.

The floor dropped away. Once again Tom felt like he was floating in nothingness. Suddenly, he remembered something. "Oh no," he yelled. "We're going back to…"

CHAPTER 10
ENCORE

"…the school talent show," Tom finished.

The mist vanished. Once again, he was standing on the wet floor of the stage. In his hand was a mop. For the moment, time was standing still, but sooner or later he would have to face the disaster that he and Zuma had caused. All the dancers in Break Quake were angry with him, and Mr Braintree had looked furious too. "Oh no," he groaned, wondering what his punishment would be. "I wish we had stayed in Australia."

"Me too," said Zuma. "I'm starving. I'd love another handful of those delicious witchetty grubs."

Tom turned to Zuma. With their quest over, the Aztec girl was dressed in her feathered headdress and blue skin paint again.

"Are you telling me you *liked* eating those things?" asked Tom. He made a face, remembering the feeling of the wriggly grubs in his mouth.

Zuma nodded. "What's not to like? They tasted just like—"

Whatever Zuma was about to say was cut off by a ground-shaking rumble of thunder. Stinging rain began to fall. Shielding his eyes with one hand, Tom looked up.

Above his head, Tlaloc's face glared down

from swirling black clouds. The rain god's
eyes were bulging with anger, his sharp teeth
gnashing together. "So, you found the third

coin," Tlaloc said. As he spoke, the thunder shook the stage again. Rain poured down harder than ever. "I am here to collect it."

Without a word, Zuma held up the chain with the golden coin.

Tom shivered as he stared at the face above him. With every coin they found, Tlaloc seemed to become more enraged. *We'd better be careful next time*, Tom thought to himself. The rain god would surely make the next quest even *more* difficult.

"You may be halfway there," Tlaloc snarled. "But you still need three more coins to win Zuma's freedom. You can be certain that you will fail."

Tlaloc disappeared in a flash of lightning. The rainstorm vanished. For a few seconds there was silence, then Tom heard another thunderous roar growing in the background.

"What's Tlaloc up to now?" he said with a groan.

"I don't think it's thunder. It's coming from out there," said Zuma, pointing to the stage curtain.

Someone backstage raised the curtain. A spotlight fell on Tom. The roaring sound increased. He gulped again, uncertain what was happening. Then he blinked in surprise. The audience was laughing, stamping their feet and cheering wildly.

"What's going on?" Tom said, gazing around.

Zuma didn't reply. She was too busy bowing to an audience that couldn't see her.

Not knowing what else to do, Tom

waved. The audience erupted into fresh
cheers. A man in the front row shouted,
"Encore! Encore!"

Mr Braintree bounded out from the
backstage area. "Let's hear it for Tom," he
bellowed. "Wasn't he brilliant?"

"But it was an accident," Tom said, looking confused.

Mr Braintree wasn't listening. "The way you knocked that bucket over and made everyone on stage slide about," he chuckled. "Very, *very* funny."

Eventually, after more cheering, the curtain dropped again.

"The audience thought that was hilarious, Tom," said Mr Braintree. "No one need know it was an accident!"

From the other side of the stage, Break Quake ran out, shouting with laughter. One of the dancers slapped Tom on the shoulder, no longer angry with him. "You've *got* to join our group," he yelled. "With a comedy routine like that, we could be on TV!"

Blushing, Tom walked off stage and into the wings.

"Looks like you stole the show," said Zuma, her eyes twinkling.

They glanced at each other and then burst out laughing. Three coins down and three to go – who knew where they would end up next?

TIME HUNTERS

TURN THE PAGE TO . . .

➜ Meet the REAL Outlaws!

➜ Find out fantastic FACTS!

➜ Battle with your GAMING CARDS!

➜ And MUCH MORE!

WHO WERE THE MIGHTIEST OUTLAWS?

Ben Hall was a *real* outlaw. Find out more about him and other famous outback outlaws!

BEN HALL was a cattle rancher in New South Wales, who gave up farming for a life of crime as a bushranger. Nicknamed Brave Ben Hall, he committed over 600 robberies, but never killed anyone. His gang once held the entire village of Canowindra hostage in a hotel and locked the police in a prison cell! In 1865 Hall was ambushed by police and shot dead as he tried to flee. He is remembered as a folk hero in many songs and stories.

OUTBACK

BEN HALL

Brain Power	290
Fear Factor	300
Bravery	380
Weapon: Bushranger Knife	280

— TOTAL **1250** —

CAPTAIN THUNDERBOLT

was really called Frederick
Ward. He was sent to
prison on Cockatoo
Island, but famously
escaped in 1863 by
swimming through
dangerous waters
to the mainland.
Giving himself the
nickname Captain Thunderbolt,
Fred formed a gang of bushrangers, including
his loyal girlfriend, Mary-Ann Bugg, and went
on a crime spree lasting nearly seven years.
He was shot dead by the police in 1870, but
his fame lives on. Today there is a road called
Thunderbolt's Way that follows the very route
he used to terrorise!

OUTBACK
CAPTAIN THUNDERBOLT

Brain Power	270
Fear Factor	290
Bravery	280
Weapon: Revolver	300

TOTAL 1140

FRANK GARDINER was born in Scotland, but moved to Australia as a child. There he became an outlaw, helping Ben Hall carry out the Lachlan Gold Escort robbery in 1862 – one of Australia's largest ever gold robberies. Although the police found most of the gold, the location of the rest remains a mystery. Frank Gardiner went to prison, but was let out early on one condition: he had to leave the country! In 1874 Frank Gardiner travelled to the United States, where he opened a saloon in California. No one knows how or when he died – or where he hid the rest of the gold!

OUTBACK

FRANK GARDINER

Brain Power	240
Fear Factor	230
Bravery	250
Weapon: Pistol	285

TOTAL 1005

NED KELLY was Australia's most notorious outlaw. Ned got an early start to his life of crime, going to jail for the first time when he was only 15! But he didn't learn his lesson – when he got out of prison, Ned continued to steal cattle and horses. His crimes turned more violent when he shot two policemen dead when they found his hideout. Over the next two years, Ned Kelly and his gang robbed banks and avoided capture. During this time, Ned wrote a famous letter to the police, complaining about their bad treatment of his family and other poor Irish Australians. The police finally caught up with Ned in 1880 and after a long shoot-out, Ned was captured and sentenced to death by hanging.

OUTBACK
NED KELLY

Brain Power	200
Fear Factor	350
Bravery	300
Weapon: Sawn-off Carbine	320

TOTAL **1170**

WEAPONS

Ned Kelly was a dab hand with a sawn-off shotgun! Find out what other weapons the Outback Outlaws used.

Musket: A long firearm meant to be fired from the shoulder, used by early European settlers.

Pistol: A small hand gun that was popular because it could be easily hidden.

Boomerang: A moon-shaped wooden tool designed to return to its owner when thrown. They were used by Aborigines for hunting, sport and entertainment and were often beautifully decorated.

Nulla Nulla: An Aboriginal club made from wattle, common in the Queensland area.

AUSTRALIAN OUTBACK TIMELINE

In OUTBACK OUTLAW Tom and Zuma go to the Australian Outback. Discover more about it in this brilliant timeline!

8000 BC
Aboriginal Australians invent the boomerang

AD 1788
Arrival of the first convicts in New South Wales.

AD 1851
Discovery of gold in New South Wales starts a gold rush

AD 1770
Captain Cook spots Botany Bay from HMS *Endeavour* and calls the land New South Wales.

AD 1812–19
Bushrangers commit crimes in Tasmania.

AD 1865
The Felons Apprehension Act allows known bushrangers to be shot and killed on sight.

AD 1878–80
The Ned Kelly Gang is at large.

AD 1863–65
Ben Hall robs travellers on the Melbourne-Sydney road.

AD 1869
Land reservations are created and Aboriginal Australians are forced to live on them.

AD 1900
Australia becomes a Commonwealth and its separate colonies become a union of states.

TIME HUNTERS TIMELINE

Tom and Zuma never know where in history they'll travel to next! Check out in what order their adventures actually happen.

10,000 BC–3000 BC

The Stone Age

AD 1427–AD 1521

The Aztec Empire

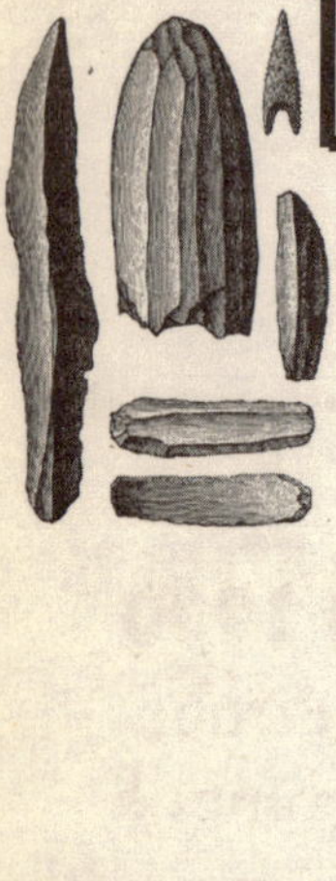

AD 1185–AD 1868

Feudal Japan

AD 1775–AD 1900

Era of the 'Wild West' in America.

AD 1492–AD 1607

First contact between Native American tribes and European settlers in America.

AD 1850–AD 1880

Bushranger outlaws become famous in Australia.

FANTASTIC FACTS

Impress your friends with these facts about
Outback Outlaws!

→ Ned Kelly was Australia's most famous
bushranger and outlaw. Many charges
were brought against him and his
notorious gang, including theft, bank
robbery, murder and even taking an
entire town captive! Kelly was eventually
hanged in Melbourne Gaol in 1880. *Yikes!*

→ Bushrangers were outlaws in Australia,
similar to highwaymen in Britain. Many
of them, like Captain Thunderbolt,
became household names.
Well, it is a great name!

➤   Many bushrangers saw themselves as Robin Hood figures, stealing from the rich to give to the poor. *Hurrah!*

➤   The first European people to arrive in Australia were a group of eight hundred convicts, transported there in 1788 as punishment for their crimes. *Better than detention!*

➤   It is still traditional for the young Aboriginal tribesmen of Australia's Outback to go 'Walkabout' – a long journey into the wilderness. It is a rite of passage that can last up to six months. *And you thought maths lessons were long!*

WHO IS THE MIGHTIEST?

Collect the Gaming Cards and play!

Battle with a friend to find out which
historical hero is the mightiest of them all!

Players: 2
Number of Cards: 4+ each

 Players start with an equal number of
cards. Decide which player goes first.

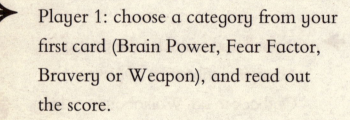 Player 1: choose a category from your
first card (Brain Power, Fear Factor,
Bravery or Weapon), and read out
the score.

 Player 2: read out the stat from the
same category on your first card.

The player with the highest score wins the round, takes their opponent's card and puts it at the back of their own pack.

 The winning player then chooses a category from the next card and play continues.

→ The game continues until one player has won all the cards. The last card played wins the title 'Mightiest hero of them all!'

OUTBACK
BEN HALL

Brain Power 290
Fear Factor 300
Bravery 380
Weapon: Bushranger Knife 280
— TOTAL **1250** —

For more fantastic games go to:
www.time-hunters.com

BATTLE THE MIGHTIEST!

Collect a new set of mighty warriors — free in every
Time Hunters book! Have you got them all?

COWBOYS

- [ ] Wyatt Earp
- [ ] Wild Bill Hickok
- [ ] Buffalo Bill
- [ ] Billy the Kid

SAMURAIS

- [ ] Lord Kenshin
- [ ] Honda Tadakatsu
- [ ] Lord Shingen
- [ ] Hattori Hanzo

OUTBACK OUTLAWS

- [ ] Ben Hall
- [ ] Captain Thunderbolt
- [ ] Frank Gardiner
- [ ] Ned Kelly

STONE AGE MEN

- ☐ Gam
- ☐ Col
- ☐ Orm
- ☐ Pag

BRAVES

- ☐ Shabash
- ☐ Crazy Horse
- ☐ Geronimo
- ☐ Sitting Bull

AZTECS

- ☐ Ahuizotl
- ☐ Zuma
- ☐ Tlaloc
- ☐ Moctezuma II

MORE MIGHTY WARRIORS!

Don't forget to collect these warriors from Tom's first adventure!

GLADIATORS

- ☐ Hilarus
- ☐ Spartacus
- ☐ Flamma
- ☐ Emperor Commodus

KNIGHTS

- ☐ King Arthur
- ☐ Galahad
- ☐ Lancelot
- ☐ Gawain

VIKINGS

- ☐ Erik the Red
- ☐ Harald Bluetooth
- ☐ Ivar the Boneless
- ☐ Canute the Great

GREEKS

- ☐ Hector
- ☐ Ajax
- ☐ Achilles
- ☐ Odysseus

PIRATES

- ☐ Blackbeard
- ☐ Captain Kidd
- ☐ Henry Morgan
- ☐ Calico Jack

EGYPTIANS

- ☐ Anubis
- ☐ King Tut
- ☐ Isis
- ☐ Tom

CHRIS BLAKE

TIME HUNTERS

FREE GAMING CARDS INSIDE

STONE AGE RAMPAGE
Battle the mightiest!

What was the Stone Age like?
Who were the Stone Age men?
What weapons did they fight with?

Join Tom and Zuma on another action-packed
Time Hunters adventure!

The magical mist cleared and Tom found
himself standing at the top of a mountain
overlooking a valley. The air was pure
and fresh, unlike anything Tom had ever
breathed before. There wasn't a person or a

building or a road anywhere to be seen.

"Great view!" said Zuma. "But where are we?"

Tom looked at the bulky fur cloak draped over Zuma's shoulders. Whenever Tlaloc sent them tumbling through time, their clothes changed to match the style of the period they were visiting. Tom was dressed in a similar cloak to Zuma. Both of them were wearing leggings made from animal hide, and furry boots stuffed with grass.

"We're definitely a long way from home," Tom said. "I think further than we've ever been before." He pointed to the black pendant hanging round her neck. "Ask your necklace and see if it can help us."

Zuma's magical pendant gave them clues to where Tlaloc had hidden each golden coin. Taking hold of the necklace, Zuma chanted the familiar question:

"Mirror, mirror, on a chain,
Can you help us? Please explain!
We are lost and must be told
How to find the coins of gold."

A riddle appeared on the surface of the black pendant:

Step back to the dawn of time;
To find the coin follow the rhyme.
Two men of stone — one large, one small;
You'll find a clue upon the wall.
Go down a path of bubbling blue;
When in doubt, to the right stay true;
Keep on past where the deer roam;
The brightest fire will lead you home.

"What does 'the dawn of time' mean?" Zuma asked, as the silvery words vanished into the depths of the pendant.

"If our clothes are anything to go by, I'd

say we're in the prehistoric era," said Tom.

"Prehis-whatty?" laughed Zuma. "That's not a word! You're making it up."

"I'm not!" said Tom.

"What does it mean then?"

"It's a very old period in time," Tom explained, remembering what his dad had told him. "Way before the Ancient Romans, Greeks and Egyptians. Way before people could even read or write."

"Hmm." Zuma frowned. "So… no computer games?"

"Not really, no," said Tom.

A sudden gust of wind whipped across the mountaintop. Tom shivered, and pulled his cloak tightly round him. "Let's get down from here," he suggested. "It'll be warmer in the valley."

"Lead the way," said Zuma.

They began to pick their way down
the jagged slope, careful not to slip on the
loose rocks. Chilli darted ahead of them,
sniffing and snuffling at the ground. The air
was still cool and crisp, but walking helped
warm Tom up. As they carried on down
the mountain, Zuma looked at her boots
admiringly.

"These shoes don't look like much," she
said. "But they're pretty comfortable. These
prehis-whatty people couldn't have been
that stupid."

"I didn't say they were stupid," said Tom.
"I just said they hadn't learned to read or
write yet."

"How about talking? Could they talk like
us?"

"No one really knows," replied Tom.
"Their words probably sounded a lot

different to ours – like a lot of huffs and grunts."

"Sounds like my old master," Zuma told him. "He used to huff and grunt all the time, especially when I burned his breakfast."

Thanks to Tlaloc's magic, whenever Tom and Zuma travelled back in time they could understand whatever language the people there spoke. Even if people round here huffed and grunted, Tom would be able to understand them. He was still worried, though. This empty world felt strange and different. Whenever Tom saw prehistoric people on the TV, they were brutish cavemen who bashed people on the head with clubs and dragged them away by their hair. Had anyone even invented fire yet? Tlaloc hadn't been joking when he'd said that this would be Tom and Zuma's toughest challenge yet.

As they came down the mountain, the ground began to level out and a line of trees appeared along a ridge. Chilli barked with delight and scooted down towards the nearest tree. The dog's nose twitched excitedly as he sniffed round the gnarled roots.

"Looks like Chilli's caught a scent of something," said Tom.

"Maybe it's Tlaloc's coin," Zuma said hopefully.

"I don't think you can smell gold."

"You don't know Chilli," Zuma told him. "He can sniff out *anything.*"

They followed the Chihuahua over to the large tree. The little dog had stopped sniffing the roots and was now looking up into the leafy branches.

"You see?" Zuma said. "The coin must be up in those branches. All we have to do is climb and get it."

Tom peered up into the shadowy tree. Something moved in the branches – but it wasn't a coin.

"Look out!" he cried.

The next moment a net dropped down from the tree, knocking Tom and Zuma off their feet and pinning them to the ground!

*

Tom and Zuma squirmed beneath the net, the prickly ropes scratching at their skin. Chilli had been caught in the net too, and was trying to gnaw his way free. But he was just as stuck as they were.

"It's no use," groaned Zuma. "We're

trapped!"

Two shadowy figures dropped down from the tree's upper branches, landing on either side of the net. Tom cried out in surprise. He tried to stand up, but the more he thrashed about, the more tangled up he got. The figures leaned in closer, peering at their catch through the gaps in the net. One was a grown man, the other a young boy.

A real live caveman, thought Tom. *And a caveboy!*

Like Tom and Zuma, their captors were wrapped in bulky fur cloaks over hide leggings. They wore furry brown hats made from some kind of animal skin, and carried rucksacks made from a hairy pelt. But it wasn't their clothes that made the breath catch in Tom's throat – it was their weapons. The man was carrying a bow and a quiver filled with arrows, as well as a copper axe. The boy had pulled a sharp dagger from his belt, and was pointing it threateningly at Tom and Zuma.

As they tried to wriggle free, Chilli had managed to gnaw a hole in the net big enough for his little body. Squeezing through the gap, he charged at the hunters, yapping furiously. To Tom's horror, the man drew the axe from his belt and swung it at Chilli. The Chihuahua darted out of the way, missing the blade by inches.

"No!" screamed Zuma. "Don't hurt him!"

The man jumped. "Goat talks?" he gasped, blinking in astonishment.

"Who are you calling a goat?" Zuma said indignantly.

The boy made a grumbling noise that

Tom realised was a chuckle. "She's not a goat, Blood-Father," he said. "She's a girl." The boy stuck his knife back into his belt. Lifting up the net, he helped Tom and Zuma out. "Sorry," he said. "We thought you were food."

Tom and Zuma scrambled clear of the net, relieved to be free from the prickly ropes. The older hunter put away his axe. He was still scowling. "What tribe you belong?" he asked curtly.

Tom scratched his head, not sure how to answer. "My tribe isn't from round here. We've come from very far away."

"From beyond the mountains?" the hunter asked suspiciously.

"Way beyond them," said Zuma. At her feet Chilli was still glaring at the hunter, giving him a warning growl. Zuma picked up the Chihuahua and gave him a hug.

As the boy began to gather the net, Tom helped him. "This is a strong net," he said, inspecting the rope. "What did you make it out of?"

"String peeled from inside of tree bark," said the boy, beaming. "I twisted the string into a length of twine, then wove it into a net."

"Cool!" said Tom.

The older hunter gave his chest a thump and grunted. "Gam," he said, then pointed a scarred finger at the boy. "This Gam's Blood-Son, Arn."

Following the man's lead, Tom thumped his own chest and said, "Tom." He then pointed to Zuma and told the hunters her name.

"Gam glad to meet Tom and Zuma,"

said Gam. He let out a heavy sigh. "But still wish you were goats."

"What is it with this guy and goats?" muttered Zuma.

"Blood-Father is upset because we haven't caught any food," Arn explained. "A new tribe led by a man called Orm has come over the mountains. For months now they have been hunting on our land and stealing our food."

"Poachers," said Tom.

Gam nodded. "Orm bad man," he said. "He kills more deer and goats than he needs. Gam can't feed his tribe if enemy kills all animals for themselves."

"We aren't part of Orm's tribe, I promise," said Zuma. "And for the record, this is Chilli." She mimicked Gam, giving Chilli's chest a little thump. "Chilli not goat, either. Chilli is friend."

"Why Tom and Zuma here if not hunting?" Gam asked.

"In a way we are hunting," Tom explained. "We've come to find something important that's been hidden somewhere. As soon as we find it we can go home."

"Gam and Arn want to go home too," said Gam. "But because of Orm, we must travel far to hunt now."

There was a sudden noise higher up the mountain, the sound of stones crunching underfoot. Tom looked up to see a goat scrambling across the slope.

"Look, Blood-Father!" pointed Arn. "A goat! A real one this time."

"Shh," said Gam, slipping his bow from his shoulder. "Loud voice frighten goat away." Keeping his eyes trained on the goat, he pulled an arrow from his quiver and nimbly placed it against the bowstring. He took aim.

But before Gam could shoot, Tom and Zuma heard a rumbling laugh. It was Tlaloc! There was a deafening thunderclap. The goat let out a terrified bleat and bounded away, sending a shower of stones tumbling down the slope.

"No move!" Gam said urgently. "No sound! No want rockfall."

But even as Tom and Zuma froze, Tlaloc let off an even louder bang of thunder that echoed round the valley. The trickle of stones started to dislodge large rocks. The rain god had created an avalanche!

"Run!" shouted Gam.

At once the hunter began racing back towards the trees. Tom and Zuma ran

after him. It was hard for them to keep
up with Gam's long strides, and they were
soon several paces behind. As they neared
the trees, Tom realised that Arn wasn't
with them. Turning round, he saw that the
prehistoric boy had stopped in his tracks, and
was looking up the mountain.

Tom gasped.

An enormous boulder was rolling straight
towards Arn. If he didn't move fast, he was
going to be squashed flat!

THE HUNT CONTINUES...

Travel through time with Tom and Zuma as they battle the mightiest warriors of the past. Will they find all six coins and win Zuma's freedom? Find out in:

Got it! ☑

Got it! ☑

Got it! ☑

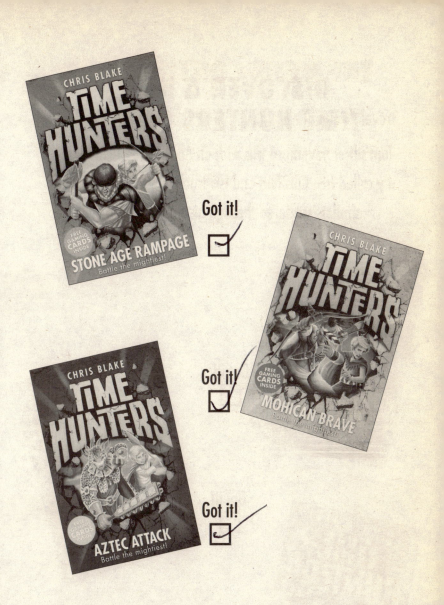

Got it!

Got it!

Got it!

Tick off the books as you collect them!

DISCOVER A NEW TIME HUNTERS QUEST!

Tom's first adventure was with an Ancient Egyptian mummy called Isis. Can Tom and Isis track down the six hidden amulets scattered through history? Find out in:

Got it! ☐

Got it! ☐

Got it! ☐